Praise for Gardner Dozois

"Gardner Dozois is one of the pre-eminent authors in the history of science fiction and fantasy. One of the strongest talents to enter the field in the last half of the century, Dozois's stories, be they set in a wildly imaginative future or the recent past, are never less than supremely literate, and profoundly human."

—Lucius Shepard

"Gardner Dozois's ear for dialogue never falters, nor does his ability to capture the essence of character in diverse situations. His vision is bleak, yet his words, in contrast, sing. Dozois is a great, neglected American writer."

—Ellen Datlow

"A story from Gardner—all too rare an event—is cause for celebration. A whole collection is a literary milestone. Gardner Dozois is one of the best writers we have. His range and power are astonishing."

—Nancy Kress

"His work is bitter, subtle, exotic, unique: science fiction for the true connoisseur."

—Joe Haldeman

"Intense, well-rendered and colorfully done . . . a careful sculptor of ideas, a sensitive observer of human responses and a narrator who cares about the way things are said."

—Roger Zelazny

"Dozois is a writer who prowls the terrain of nightmare, bringing back strange loves and horrors you will not soon forget. Included here are some of the most imaginative and poignant concepts in recent fiction, incarnated in a sustained, almost tangible realness that holds your eyes to the page."

—James Tiptree, Jr.

More Praise for Gardner Dozois

"A unique writing talent who speaks with a distinctive voice. He is a writer's writer, and what's more, he is a reader's writer."

—Ben Bova

"Gardner Dozois is one of the most powerful writers of his generation."
—Mike Resnick

"Gardner Dozois is one of the best short-fiction writers alive."
—Andy Duncan

"One of the very best short story writers ever to have worked in the genre. A precise, lyrical stylist, he is also a deep, humane writer who can tease the humor out of tragedy."

—Jack Dann

"Rich, multicolored, passionate, provacative and illuminating . . . Gardner Dozois is the finest stylist of his generation."

—S.P. Somtow

"My generation of science fiction writers has produced relatively few authenic masters of the short form. Gardner Dozois is one of them.

—William Gibson

"One of the most gifted writers in the United States."
—Robert Silverberg

"Dozois can create as well as he can edit, a skill which is not always available to editors."

—SFSite